U $\quad$ ᴺᴳ

HERTS SCHOOLS LIBRARY SERVICE

000000395065

By the same author

My Best Fiend
The Fiend Next Door
Holiday with the Fiend
Trouble with the Fiend

(Gazelles)
Ursula Bear
Ursula Camping
Ursula Dancing
Ursula Exploring
Ursula Flying
Ursula Sailing

(Cartwheels)
Ursula at the Zoo
Ursula by the Sea
Harry's Aunt

URSULA RIDING

by
SHEILA LAVELLE
Illustrated by Thelma Lambert

HAMISH HAMILTON
LONDON

First published in Great Britain 1985
by Hamish Hamilton Children's Books
27 Wrights Lane, London W8 5TZ
Copyright © 1985 by Sheila Lavelle
Illustrations copyright © 1985 by Thelma Lambert

Reprinted 1987

British Library Cataloguing in Publication Data
Lavelle, Sheila
    Ursula riding.—(Gazelle books)
    I. Title   II. Series
    823'.914   (J)   PZ7

    ISBN 0–241–11426–8

Filmset in Baskerville by
Katerprint Co Ltd, Oxford
Printed in Great Britain at the
University Press, Cambridge

HERTFORDSHIRE
LIBRARY SERVICE

No. 0395065

Class

Supplier   Price   Date

Chapter One

Ursula woke up one sunny Saturday morning to find the delicious smell of frying bacon drifting up the stairs. She ran down to the kitchen, flung her arms round Aunt Prudence's waist and gave her a big squeeze.

"Well," said Aunt Prudence, blinking in surprise. "Somebody's in a good mood this morning."

Ursula sat down at the table and began to spoon up cornflakes as fast as she could.

"It's the fair today," she said. "I've been looking forward to it for weeks. You can't have forgotten."

"Don't talk with your mouth full," said Aunt Prudence, breaking an egg into the frying pan. "What's all this fuss about a village fair, anyway? You've never been excited about it before."

"They've never had a performing bear before," said Ursula. She jumped off her chair and danced round the kitchen. "A proper, trained, performing bear. From a circus. Mr Blomeyer fixed it all up. And guess who's going to help him look after it? ME!"

2

Aunt Prudence smiled and shook her head. "You and your bears," she said. "You're as daft as a dumpling about them. I'd rather have a game of bingo myself." She pushed a plate of bacon and eggs across the table. "You'll need a decent breakfast if you're going to be out all day. And you'll want to take a picnic lunch, as well, I suppose."

After breakfast Ursula put on her new white dress with the poppies on it, and then helped Aunt Prudence to pack the picnic basket. The last thing they put in was an enormous sticky

currant bun, filled with a mixture of porridge oats and honey. A present for the performing bear.

"See you at teatime, Auntie," said Ursula, kissing Aunt Prudence's cheek. She picked up the basket and set off to call for her friend, Mrs Martinez.

Mrs Martinez lived in the untidiest house you ever saw. She liked painting pictures or playing her flute better than cleaning or polishing, so she never minded when Ursula forgot to wipe her feet. And she never, ever nagged about sticky fingermarks, or biscuit crumbs, or blobs of ice-cream on the carpet.

Ursula pushed open the gate, and found her friend in the front garden, looking very pretty in her best straw hat with the velvet ribbon. Mr Blomeyer was there too, looking worried and upset, and waving a telegram in his hand. Ursula knew something terrible had happened as soon as she saw his face.

"Oh dear," said Mrs Martinez, taking Ursula's hand. "You tell her, Paul. I just can't."

Ursula looked at Mr Blomeyer, who cleared his throat as if he had a frog in it.

"It's the performing bear, Ursula," he said sadly. "The circus at Deadleigh Green can't send him, after all. He hurt his leg doing a cartwheel in last night's show. So the whole thing's off, I'm afraid."

6

Ursula sat down with a bump on Mrs Martinez's front doorstep. She felt so disappointed she could have cried.

Chapter Two

Mr Blomeyer pushed the telegram into his pocket.

"I suppose we'd better be getting along to the fairground," he sighed. "Put up a notice or something. An awful lot of people will be disappointed."

"Nebber mind," said Mrs Martinez, who was Spanish and always had trouble with the letter V. "They'll still hab a happy time. Pony rides and coconut throwing and ice-cream and cheeps and warm dogs, yes?"

"Hot dogs," said Mr Blomeyer gloomily. And he began to walk towards the gate.

Ursula jumped up, her eyes as round as dinner plates.

"Wait," she said, her voice coming out all squeaky. "What about me? I could be the performing bear."

The two grown-ups gazed at Ursula for a moment. Then suddenly they began to smile, for they both knew that Ursula had a strange and wonderful secret. With a simple magic spell, Ursula could turn herself from an ordinary little girl into a real, live bear.

"It's a great idea," said Ursula, jumping up and down with excitement. "I've already got the right sort of magic bun with me. It'll be as easy as pie."

Mrs Martinez hugged Ursula in delight and the two of them did a jig together round the lilac tree. But Mr Blomeyer looked doubtful.

"It's not safe," he said. "What if something goes wrong? What if you can't change back again? What if your aunt should find out? I don't like it at all."

Mrs Martinez took his arm and gave it a shake.

"Now, Paul," she coaxed. "Don't be an old sportspoil. Theenk about all those disappointed children."

Mr Blomeyer took a deep breath. "All right," he said quickly. "We'll do it. Swallow that bun, Ursula."

Ursula didn't need telling twice. She sat down under the lilac tree and unpacked the currant bun from her basket. And while she ate it she recited the words of the spell.

"I'm a bear, I'm a bear, I'm a bear," she said. "I'm a bear, I'm a bear, I'm a bear."

Her two friends watched in silent wonder as Ursula slowly disappeared. And in her place was a small, fat, brown bear, grinning up at them with black twinkling eyes.

Chapter Three

Ursula peeped out of the car window and waved her paws at the crowd as Mr Blomeyer drove through the gate into the packed fairground. Hundreds of people thronged the meadow, and gaily-coloured flags and streamers fluttered everywhere in the breeze. Small children ran about in fancy dress, while mums and dads and grandmas and grandpas tried their luck at the coconut shy or the hoop-la. The village band played merrily away in a corner of the field, ponies trotted up and down giving rides, and everybody seemed to be having a wonderful time.

"The bear! It's here!" somebody called out, as Mr Blomeyer lifted Ursula from the car, and in no time at all they were surrounded by an excited crowd. Mr Blomeyer had to perch Ursula high on his shoulder and force a way through, while Mrs Martinez followed closely behind.

In the middle of the field stood a marquee, with a notice on the doorway saying, 'DON'T MISS THE

PERFORMING BEAR. 11.30 A.M.'
Ursula felt a strange fluttering in her
stomach as Mr Blomeyer carried her
inside, and she clutched his head so
tightly with her paws that he could
hardly see where he was going.

"Good luck, Ursula," he whispered, lifting her up onto the edge of the lighted stage, and the waiting crowd began to cheer and stamp their feet when they saw that the show was about to begin.

Ursula felt alone and shy and very small on that great big stage in front of all those people. She pressed her furry paws together to stop them trembling, and the crowd went quiet as the music began. Ursula took a deep breath. Then the audience gasped as the little brown bear suddenly did one backward somersault after another, right round the edge of the stage.

After that Ursula danced a polka and juggled with skittles. She did handstands and cartwheels and somersaults. She rode a tricycle and stood on her head, and she even did some disco-dancing that she'd learnt from watching Top of the Pops.

The crowd loved every minute of it. They clapped and cheered and whistled and stamped their feet and threw buns at the stage. When the music stopped and Ursula made her final bow, they would not let her go. They shouted for more, and still more, until Mr Blomeyer had to climb onto the stage and hold up his hand.

"That's all, ladies and gentlemen," he said, smiling. "This little bear deserves a rest."

The audience, after a few more cheers and another burst of applause, made their way out of the tent. Mr Blomeyer grabbed Ursula's paw and shook it hard.

"Well done, Ursula," he said. "That was some performance."

Ursula flopped down on her back on the stage, feeling quite worn out.

"Poor leetle thing," said Mrs Martinez. "Lie here and rest while Paul and I get you some nice beefburgers and cheeps, yes? Then you can turn back into yourself again and enjoy the rest of the fair."

Ursula closed her eyes thankfully as her friends went out of the marquee.

Chapter Four

Ursula awoke with a start to hear voices muttering somewhere close by.

"Grab him quick," somebody was saying. Ursula only had time to catch a glimpse of two youths in jeans and leather jackets before she found herself being roughly bundled into a smelly sack and carried away.

Ursula growled and kicked and struggled and fought, but none of it was any use. The thick sack muffled her voice and the loud music of the brass band completely drowned her cries. Nobody in the crowd noticed the two kidnappers as they hurried towards the gate carrying a wriggling, bouncing sack between them.

The breath was knocked from Ursula's body as she was dumped suddenly down on something hard. Then she heard a door slam and the sound of an engine starting up. The floor rattled and jolted beneath her and Ursula's heart thumped in her chest as she realised what was happening. She was in the back of some sort of van, being driven away from the fairground, and she might never see her friends again.

Ursula could hear the kidnappers arguing as they drove along, and she pricked up her furry ears.

"What d'you want to steal a bear for, anyway, Dobbsy?" a surly voice was saying. "What we gonna do with it?"

"Sell it, stupid," came the reply. "There's that circus over at Deadleigh Green, right? Bet you they'll give us at least a hundred quid for it. 'Specially when they see what it can do."

Ursula groaned miserably. It was hot and stuffy in the sack and she could hardly breathe. She didn't want to be sold to a circus and spend the rest of her life in a cage. And what would poor Mr Blomeyer say when he

24

found her missing? He would blame
himself for the whole thing. Worn out
by her struggles, Ursula huddled in
the sack, waiting to see what would
happen next. There was nothing else
she could do.

Chapter Five

After a while the van stopped and
Ursula felt herself being lifted out.
She was carried a short distance and
then at last the top of the sack was
unfastened. Ursula stood up, wob-
bling a bit and blinking in the light.
She gazed about her with big round
eyes, and for a moment she forgot to
be scared.

Ursula was in the circus, in the big top itself, right in the middle of the sawdust ring. A team of six black Shetland ponies were rehearsing for the afternoon show, and a group of trapeze artists swooped and soared high above her head.

"It doesn't look like a trained bear to me," a voice said, and Ursula looked round. A tall man with enormous ginger whiskers and shiny black boots was talking to the two kidnappers.

"Honest, Mr Baldi," one of them said. "It can do gymnastics, juggling, dancing, you name it."

"Show me," said Mr Baldi, prodding Ursula's fat tummy with the end of his whip. Then he roared in

delight as Ursula did three backward somersaults in a row.

"Bravo! Molto bravo!" he shouted. Ursula gave a little bow. Then she pointed a paw at the ponies, still waiting patiently near the exit.

"A bear riding a pony?" muttered Mr Baldi, his eyes gleaming. "What a sensation!" He quickly led the smallest pony to the centre of the ring and

helped Ursula into the saddle. He put the reins into her paws and fixed the stirrups so that her short legs could reach. Then he slapped the pony's rump and stood back.

"Off you go," he said.

Ursula knew what to do. She gave the pony a good nudge with her heels and set off round the edge of the ring. Round and round they went, first at a trot, then at a canter, while Mr Baldi stood in the middle clapping his hands and the two youths stared in amazement.

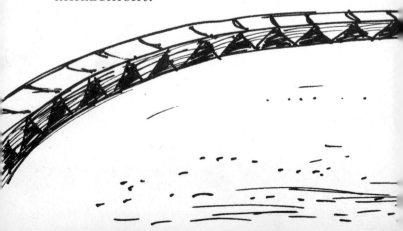

Ursula urged the pony on, faster and faster, until he was in full gallop. Then, before anyone knew what was happening, she galloped the pony straight through the exit, down the canvas tunnel, and out into the open air.

They flew past the ticket office,
where a queue was already forming
for the afternoon show, and the lady
cashier's mouth fell open at the sight.
Ursula heard shouting and running

feet behind her, and then the sound of
the van starting up.

"Jump!" she growled at the gallant
pony, steering him off the road. She

33

dug her heels in hard, and the pony
sailed over the low hedge and set off
at a fast gallop across the open fields
towards the fair.

Chapter Six

Mr Blomeyer paced up and down outside the marquee, mopping his brow and muttering to himself.

"I knew we shouldn't have let her do it," he said. "It's all my fault."

Mrs Martinez, still carrying Ursula's carton of beefburgers and chips, looked as if she were about to cry.

"What are we going to do, Paul?" she said in a small voice.

"I'll make an announcement," said Mr Blomeyer. "Somebody may have seen something." He set off towards the bandstand, with Mrs Martinez hurrying along after him.

Mr Blomeyer asked the band to stop playing for a moment and spoke into the microphone. His voice crackled out through the loudspeakers and the crowd stopped their merrymaking to listen.

"Your attention, please, ladies and gentlemen. Our performing bear has disappeared. If anyone has any information will they please come forward."

There was a short silence while

everybody looked at one another in dismay. Nobody knew anything about it, and they all shook their heads.

Suddenly the sound of galloping hooves rang out in the lane. Everybody gasped in astonishment as a black Shetland pony galloped wildly through the gate into the meadow, its tail flying in the wind. Riding on the pony's back was a small brown bear,

holding tightly to the reins with both paws. The pony skidded to a halt in front of the bandstand, and Ursula leapt off its back straight into the arms of the delighted Mr Blomeyer.

Everybody was pleased to see her safe and sound, and in no time at all the fair was back in full swing. Mr Blomeyer and Mrs Martinez hurried Ursula to the empty marquee, where they wasted no time in feeding the little bear on the almost cold beefburgers and chips.

"Raeb a m'I, raeb a m'I, raeb a m'I," growled Ursula. "Raeb a m'I, raeb a m'I, raeb a m'I." And before you could say Winnie-the-Pooh, she had turned back into herself again.

"Well, thank heavens that's over,"

breathed Mr Blomeyer in relief, when Ursula had finished telling the whole story. "I've never been so worried in my life. Ursula, I want you to promise me that you'll never turn into a bear again."

Ursula looked at the anxious faces of her two friends.

"All right. I promise," she said. But she quickly crossed her fingers behind her back, so the promise wouldn't count.